THE POTATO CHILD AND OTHERS

MRS. CHARLES J. WOODBURY

THE POTATO CHILD

It was certain that Elsie had a very hard and solitary life.

When Miss Amanda had selected her from among the girls at "The Home," the motherly matron felt sorry.

"She is a tender-hearted little thing, and a kind word goes a great way with Elsie."

Miss Amanda looked at the matron as if she were speaking Greek, and said nothing. It was quite plain that few words, either kind or unkind, would pass Miss Amanda's lips. But "The Home" was more than full, and Miss Amanda Armstrong was a person well known as the leading dressmaker in the city, a person of some money; not obliged to work now if she didn't wish to. "If cold, she is at least perfectly just," they all said.

So Elsie went to work for Miss Amanda, and lived in the kitchen. She waited on the door, washed the dishes, cleaned the vegetables, and set the table (Miss Amanda lived alone, and ate in the kitchen). Every Friday she swept the house. Her bed was in a little room in the back attic.

When she came, Miss Amanda handed her a dress and petticoat, and a pair of shoes. "These are to last six months," she said, "and see you keep yourself clean." She gave her also one change of stockings and underclothes.

"Here is your room; you do not need a light to go to bed by, and it is not healthy to sleep under too many covers."

It wasn't so much what Miss Amanda did to her, for she never struck her, nor in any way ill-treated her; nor was it so much what she said, for she said almost nothing. But she said it all in commands, and the loving little Elsie was just driven into herself.

She had had a darling mother, full of love and tenderness, and Elsie would say to herself, "I must not forget the things mama told me, 'Love can never die, and kind words can never die.'" But she had no one to love, and she never heard any kind words; so she was a bit worried. "I shall forget how kind words sound, and I shall forget how to love," sighed the little girl.

She used to long for a doll or cat or something she could call her own and talk to. She asked Miss Amanda, who said "No." She added, "I have no money to give for such foolishness as a doll, and a cat would eat its head off."

Miss Amanda had been blessed with no little-girl time. When she was young, she always had been forced to work hard, and she thought it was no worse for Elsie than it had been for herself. I don't suppose it was; but one looking in on these two could not but feel for both of them.

Elsie would try to talk to herself a little at night, but it was cheerless. Then she would lift up her knee, and draw the sheet about it for a hood, and call it a little girl. She named it Nancy Pullam, and would try to love that; but it almost broke her back when she tried to hug Nancy. "Oh, if I had something to be good to"! she said.

So she began greeting the ladies, when she opened the door, with a cheerful little "Good morning" or "Good afternoon."

"I wouldn't do that," said Miss Amanda, "it looks forward and pert. It is their place to say 'Good morning,' not yours. You have no occasion to speak to your betters, and, anyway, children should be seen and not heard."

One day, a never-forgotten day, she went down cellar to the bin of potatoes to select some for dinner. She was sorting them over and laying out all of one size, when she took up quite a long one, and lo! it had a little face on it and two eyes and a little hump between for a nose and a long crack below that made a very pretty mouth.

Elsie looked at it joyfully. "It will make me a child," she said, "no matter if it has no arms or legs; the face is everything."

She carefully placed it at the end of the bin, and whenever she could slip away without neglecting her work would run down cellar and talk softly to it.

But one day her potato-child was gone! Elsie's heart gave a big jump, and then fell like lead, and seemed to lie perfectly still; but it commenced to beat again, beat and ache, beat and ache!

She tried to look for the changeling; but the tears made her so that she couldn't see very well; and there were so many potatoes! She looked every moment she had a chance all the next day, and cried a great deal. "I can never be real happy again," she thought.

"Don't cry any more," said Miss Amanda, "it does not look well when you open the door for my customers. You have enough to eat and wear; what more do you want?"

"Something to love," said Elsie, but not very loud.

She tried not to cry again, and then she felt worse not-to shed tears, when, perhaps, her dear little potato-child was eaten up.

Two days after, as she was still searching, a little piece of white paper in the far dark corner attracted her attention. She went over and lifted it up. Behind it was a hole, and partly in and partly out of the hole lay her potato-child. I think a rat had dragged it out of the bin. She hugged it to her heart, and cried for joy.

"Oh, my darling, you have come back to me, you have come back!" And then it seemed as if the pink eyes of the potato-child looked up into Elsie's in affectionate gratitude; and it became plain to Elsie that her child loved her. She was so thankful that she even kissed the little piece of white paper. "If it hadn't been for you I would never have found my child. I mean to keep you always," she said, and she wrapped it about her potato-child, and put them in her bosom. "We must never be parted again," she murmured.

At supper, with many misgivings, she unwrapped her treasure for Miss Amanda, and asked if she could keep it as her own. "I won't eat any potato for dinner tomorrow if you will give me this," she said.

"Well," answered Miss Amanda, "I don't know as it will do any harm; why do you want it?"

"It is my potato-child. I want to love it."

"See you lose no time, then," said Miss Amanda.

And afterward, Elsie never called the potato it, but always "my child."

She found a fragment of calico, large enough for a dress and skirt, with enough over, a queer, three-cornered piece, which she pinned about the unequal shoulders for a shawl. Upon the bonnet she worked for days.

All this sewing was a great joy to her. Last of all, she begged a bit of frayed muslin from the sweepings for a night-dress. Then she could undress her baby every night.

She must have heard a tiny tuber-voice, for she said, "Now I can never forget the sound of loving words, and the world is full of joy."

Elsie had a candle-box in her room, with the cover hung on hinges. It served the double purpose of a trunk and a seat. She put her child's clothes and the scrap of white paper in this box. In the daytime she let her child sit upon the window-sill so she could see the blue sky; but when the weather grew colder she took her down to the kitchen each morning, lest she should suffer.

Sometimes, Miss Amanda watched her closely. "She does her work well, but she is a queer thing. She makes me uneasy," she thought.

Christmas was coming. Elsie and her mother had always loved Christmas, and had invariably given some gift to each other. After their stockings were hung side by side, Christmas Eve, her mother would take her in her lap and tell her the Christmas story. So now it was a great mercy for Elsie that she had her child to work for.

One day, when she had scrubbed the pantry floor unusually clean, Miss Amanda gave her the privilege of the rag barrel. This resulted in a new Christmas suit of silk and velvet for baby; and this she made.

When Elsie left "The Home" the matron had given her a little needle-book containing a spool of thread and thimble for a good-by present. These now came into good play. She used the lamp shears to cut with.

When all was done the babe looked beautiful, except that it had no stockings. It had not even legs. "I'll make her a wooden leg, and let her be a cripple, then I shall love her all the better."

But after she had made the leg, and a very good one, too, she hadn't the heart to break the skin of her child, and push it in.

"I'll make the stockings without legs," she said, and so she did.

Elsie was very careful never to let her child see, or mention before her, how busy she was for Christmas.

She felt very sorry for Miss Amanda, and wished she had something to give her, but she could think of nothing except the piece of white paper she found with her potato-child. The afternoon before Christmas she took it from the candle-box, and smoothed it out upon the cover. It had some writing upon one side. Elsie thought it was very pretty writing—it had so many flourishes. Elsie could not read it, of course, but she hoped Miss Amanda would like it.

How should she give it to her? She didn't dare hand it to her outright, and she was certain Miss Amanda wouldn't hang any stocking; so just before dark she slipped into Miss Amanda's sleeping-room, and laid it on the brown cushion just in front of the mirror.

When Elsie had finished her work she went to her room, pinned her child's stocking to the foot of the bed and slyly tucked in the new suit she had made. Her own stockings lay flat upon the floor. Her breath caught a little bit as she noticed them. "But it doesn't matter," she said, "parents never care for themselves if they can give their children pleasure."

She crept into bed and took her child on her arm. The night was very cold. The frost made mysterious noises on the roof in the nail-holes and on the glass. She went to bed early because the kitchen was so cold. She thought "we can talk in bed." The lock of her door was broken, and she could not shut it tight. Through this the air came chilly.

Miss Amanda put on her flannel wrapper and her bed-slippers and sat down before the open fire in her sleeping-room. Some way she couldn't keep her thoughts from that little back attic room. She went into the hall, silently up the stairs, and stood outside the door. Elsie was talking softly, but Miss Amanda could hear every word, thanks to the broken lock.

"I have much to tell you to-night, dear child," she heard the waif say, "the whole story of the Christmas Child. It was years ago. His mother was very young, I guess about twice as old as I am. They hadn't any house; they were in a barn. I think there were no houses to rent in that town. But she fixed a little cradle for Him in the feed-box, and wrapped Him in long clothes, as I do you, my darling. The angels sang a new song for Him. A new star shone in the East for Him. Some men with sheep came to visit Him, and some rich men brought Him lovely presents. My mother told me all these things, and I mustn't forget them; it helps me to remember to tell it to you. So now, this lovely Christmas Child was born in a little bit of a town, the town of — oh, my child" — with a mournful cry — "I've forgotten the name of the town! I used to say it to my mother — it's the town of, the town of — I can't remember."

Miss Amanda could hear her crying a little softly.

"Never mind," she said presently. "I am very sorry; I have not told the story often enough. I wish I had some one to teach me a little, but perhaps it don't make so much difference if I have forgotten the name of the town. He came to teach us. Sure I won't forget that. Love can never die. That's the present He gave to everybody. So if nobody else gives us a Christmas present, we always have the one He gave us."

Silence for a little.

"I am very sorry for Miss Amanda, dear. She has no child to love. She has a very sad and lonely life."

Her teeth chattered a little. "It seems like a very cold night; the covers are quite thin, but we can never really suffer while our hearts are so warm. I'm glad you feel real well, and are just as plump as ever, but your little skin is just one bit wrinkled. You are not going to take cold or be sick? Oh, I couldn't give you up! I should miss you so much, you happy, good little child."

Miss Amanda heard a kiss. "Good-night, dear. I'm so tired. God bless us all, and help us to remember Miss Amanda, and let her find her present to-night."

Miss Amanda crept back to her warm room, and waited until she was sure the child was fast asleep. Then she took a down quilt off the foot of her own bed, picked up her candle, and retraced her way up-stairs.

She softly dropped the comforter upon Elsie. She heard, as a sort of echo, a soft sigh of content. Miss Amanda waited a moment, then shading the candle with one hand, she looked at the sleeping child.

The face was pale and thin. The lashes lay dark upon the white cheeks. They were quite wet; but, pressed close to them, and carefully covered by little, toil-hardened hands, was the grotesque potato in its white night-gown.

Miss Amanda was surprised by a queer click in her throat, and hurried out of the room.

She stood before her fire, candle in hand, and bitterly compressed her lips. She hopes "I'll find my Christmas present to-night. Who will send it to me, and what will it be? Whom do I care for, and who cares for me? No one. Not one human being."

She crossed the room, and, placing her candle upon the dressing-table, gazed at herself in the glass. "I am growing old, old and hard, and perfectly friendless."

But why that start and cry? There before her eyes, in the big, flourishing, boyish handwriting so well remembered, she reads: "Our love can never die. We have nothing in the world except each other, dear sister, and no matter what may come, our love can never change."

She snatched up the paper and threw herself into a chair.

"Where did it come from"? she cried. "What evil genius placed it here this night? Haven't I, years ago, torn and destroyed every word that wretched boy ever wrote me?"

She tossed her arms over her head, and rocked back and forth, and groaned aloud. She could not help her thoughts now, or keep them from going back over the past. Her heart softened as she remembered, and the scalding tears fell.

She was only a child, not much older than the one up-stairs, when her dying mother had placed her baby-brother in her arms, saying:

"He is all I have to leave you, Amanda. I know you love him. Don't ever be harsh or unforgiving to him."

How had she kept her trust? She had loved him. She had worked early and worked late for him. She had given up everything; but she had been ill-repaid.

"Ill," do I say? Verily, is this not true of Love: that it brings its own blessedness?

The fire burned low, and the room settled cold and still. She seemed to feel a pair of boyish arms about her neck and a boy's rough kiss upon her cheek.

When she was but a young woman she had moved to the big city, and started her dressmaker's shop, so that he could have a better chance at school. What a loving boy he was! So full of fun!

The wind whistled outside. She thought it was he, and she heard him again: "You're my handsome sister. Not one of the fellows have as handsome a sister as I."

How proud she had felt when she had started him off to college. "It only means a few years of a little harder work, and then I'll see my boy able to take his stand with anybody."

But now she wept and groaned afresh. "Oh, how could he treat me so, how could he! The wretched disgrace!"

He had been expelled. The president's letter was severe; but the young man's letter regretted it as only a boyish prank. He was sorry. He had never expected anything so serious would come of it. He deserved the disgrace. It only hurt him through his love for her. But only forgive him, and he would show her what he could yet do.

What had he done?

He had tied a calf to the president's door-bell.

She remembered her answer to this letter, asking for her forgiveness. It stood before her, written in characters of flame.

Had she in this been harsh to the boy, the only legacy her dying mother had to leave her?

"Never speak to me, nor see my face again. You have disgraced yourself and me."

It was not so long a letter but that she could easily remember it.

Afterward, the president himself had written again to her. He thought he had been too hasty. It was truly only a boy's prank. It was, of course, ungentlemanly, but the trick was played on All-Fool's Night, and that should have had greater weight than it did. The faculty were willing, after proper apologies were made, to excuse it, and take her brother back.

Where was her brother? He could not be found, and not one word had she heard of him since she sent that dreadful letter. He might be dead. Oh, how often she thought that! Now she wrung her hands and covered her wet cheeks with them. Her hair fell about her shoulders, as she shook in her agony of remorse.

What noise is this? the door-bell pealing through the silent house. Again and again it rings.

She did not hear this bell. She was listening to another, and how it rang! Louder and louder, how it rang, and well it might, with a calf jumping about, trying to get away from it. Even in all her misery — so near together are the ecstasies of emotion — she laughed aloud and then shuddered at the thought that she should never again hear any noise quite so loud as this of the past.

Then she felt in the silent, chill room a tattered presence, a little half-frozen hand upon her own. She turned her streaming eyes, and they were met by the big, wide eyes of Elsie.

"Miss Amanda, didn't you hear the door-bell ringing? There is something — no, there is somebody — waiting down-stairs for you."

Half dazed, half afraid, ashamed of her tears, Miss Amanda left the room, led by the child as by an unearthly presence into an unearthly presence.

Who was this bearded man that folded her in his strong, true arms?

"I have so much to tell you, dear child. I am such a happy little girl. Miss Amanda's dear brother has come home. She is so happy, and she loves him so much. And, oh darling, they both love me! And it was all you! You did it all! Oh, there is no knowing how much good one sweet, loving, contented potato-child can do in a house."

A STORY THAT NEVER ENDS

Tommy was very angry. He rushed up-stairs and into his mother's room, utterly forgetting his knock or "Am I welcome, mother?"

"Bang!" echoed the door behind him with a noise that resounded over the whole house. Why he was angry was plain enough. His eye was black, nose bleeding, coat torn, collar hanging. His mother took it off as he bent over the wash-bowl.

"Oh, Tommy," she said, "you've been fighting again."

"Well, mother," he exclaimed, "what do you expect me to do? That Bob Sykes threw rocks at me again and called me names. He said I was—"

"Hush," said his mother, "you only grow more angry as you speak. Is it hard for you now to remember the rule, 'The good things about others, the naughty things about yourself'?"

"Good! There is nothing good about him. I hate him. I wish he was dead, I do. I wish I could kill him."

Sternly his mother took him by the arm and led him before the mirror. One look at the face he saw there silenced him.

"To all intents and purposes you have killed him. 'Whosoever hateth his brother is a murderer.' You cannot but remember who said it, Tommy. It is late in the afternoon. The sun is going down. To-morrow is His birthday. Hadn't you better forgive Bob?"

"The sun may go down and the sun may come up for all I care," he answered, "I'll never forgive him."

Without further word his mother bathed his heated face and led him to her bed. "Lie down and rest," she said, "you are over excited. Quiet will help you."

He lay and looked at her as she sat quietly and gravely at her work under the Picture. Ever since he could remember, her chair at this hour of the day had been in that corner, and low over it had always hung, just as it hung now, that Picture so often explained to him, "The Walk to Emmaus." How calm and quiet his mother was; and the room, how still and cool after that crowded street! Shutting his aching eyes he could see it again now; the swearing mob of boys and men shoving him on, their brutal faces and gestures, the quarrel, the blows — those he had given and taken — he felt them again, and the burning choke of the final grip and wrestle.

Oh, how his head throbbed and ached! It seemed as if the blood would burst through.

He opened his eyes again. The room was growing darker. He almost forgot his pain for a few moments, noticing how the sunlight was straightened to a narrow lane which reached from the extreme southern end of the window to the floor in front of his mother's chair. He watched the last rays as they slowly left the floor and stole up her dress to her lap and her breast, leaving all behind and below in shadow. Now they had reached her face. It was bent over her work. Well he knew that was some Christmas gift, may be for him, — some Christmas gift, and to-morrow was Christmas! He looked again to see if he could discover what she was making, but the light had left her now, and had risen to the Picture.

Queer picture that it was! What funny clothes those men wore! Those long gabardines, mother had called them, reaching almost to the ground; shoes that showed the toes, and hoods for hats. One of them had none. How closely they looked at him!. They didn't even see which way they were going, and what a long way it was, stretching out there, dusty and hot.

The room was quite dark now save for the light on the narrow road there. What was yonder little village in the distance? What kind of a place was Emmaus? His mother had told him about it; only one street, a long and narrow one; and very few trees; and one or two trading shops only; and the houses low and flat-roofed, with no glass in them; and the sun shining down hot and straight between them,—and (oh, how his head ached!) he was out there looking for Bob Sykes. Maybe that was he lying on this rude bench with the low cedar-bush over it. If it were, he would settle matters with him quick. He would show him—but it wasn't Bob, it was only a sheep-dog asleep. So Tommy turned away and walked slowly along the middle of the street. His face burned with the heat of the sun on his bruises. He was very thirsty. Climbing a little hill over which the road lay, he saw on the other side of it another boy coming toward him. He was rather a peculiar looking boy, with a face thoughtful but pleasant. He was carrying a heavy sheepskin bag over his shoulder. Tommy determined to ask him if he knew where there was some water.

"Hello," he said, as the boy drew near.

The boy stopped and smiled at Tommy without making reply.

"Where are you going?" said Tommy.

"I am carrying this bag of tools to my father," the boy answered.

"Do you live here?" asked Tommy. "It doesn't seem like much of a place."

"No," said the boy, "it isn't much of a place, but I live here."

"What sort of tools have you got in your bag? Who is your father?"

"My father is a carpenter," answered the boy.

Tommy gave a long, low whistle. "A carpenter! Why my father owns a store, and we live in one of the best houses in town. Fairfield is the name of my town."

The boy seemed neither to notice the whistle nor the brag; but, allowing the bag to slip from his shoulders to the ground, stood, still smiling, before Tommy.

Tommy, who somehow had forgotten his pain and thirst, felt embarrassed for a moment. He never before had made that announcement without its awakening at least a little sensation, even if it were no more than a boast in return.

"This is a dull old town," he finally said. "Many jolly boys around?"

"A good many," answered the boy.

"Do you get any time to play? I suppose though, you don't—you have to work most of the time," added Tommy, encouragingly.

"I work a good deal," said the boy. "I get time to play, however. I like it."

"Which, the work or the play?"

"Both."

"Well," said Tommy after a pause, "do you ever have any trouble with the boys you play with?"

"No," said the boy, "I don't think I do."

"Well, you must be a queer sort of a boy! Now, there's Bob Sykes,—perhaps you've noticed that my eye is hurt, and my face scratched some. Well, we had a little difficulty just a few moments ago; he insulted me, and I won't take an insult from any one. And I told him to shut up his mouth, and he sassed me back, and called me names, and said I was stuck up and thought I was better than the other boys, and he'd show me that I wasn't. Of course, I wouldn't stand that, so I've had a fight,—and it isn't the first one either."

"Yes," said the boy, "I know that. I feel very sorry for Bob. He hasn't any mother to go to, you know. He had to wash the blood and dirt off his face as best he could at the town pump; and then wait around the streets until his father came from work. It is pretty hard for a boy to have no place to lay his head."

"Why, do you know Bob Sykes?" asked Tommy.

"Yes," answered the boy, "I've been with him a good deal."

"Queer now," mused Tommy. "I don't remember of ever seeing you around. But now tell me what you would have done if he had provoked you, and insulted you, too?"

"I would have forgiven him," answered the boy.

"Well, I did. There was one spell I just started in and forgave him every day for a week, that was seven times."

"I would have forgiven him seventy times seven."

"That is just what my mother always says. Perhaps you know my mother?"

"She knows me, too," replied the boy.

"That is odd. I didn't think she knew any of the boys Bob knows."

"Bob does not know me," replied the boy; "I know him."

Just then Tommy's attention was attracted by a flock of little brown birds passing over their heads. One of the birds flew low and fluttered as if wounded, and fell in the dust near, where it lay beating its little wings, panting and dying. The boy tenderly picked it up.

"Somebody's hit him with a sling-shot," said Tommy, carelessly.

The boy smoothed the bruised wing, and straightened the crushed and broken body. The bird ceased fluttering.

"I'm most sorry," said Tommy, "I didn't forgive Bob. It makes me feel bad, what you told me about his having no home. Now, mother is something like you. She don't mind one's being poor. Why, if I took Bob home with me, mother wouldn't seem to see his clothes and ragged shoes. She'd just talk to him and treat him like he was the best dressed boy in town. There's Bill Logan came home to dinner with me once. Mother made me ask him. He is a real poor boy; has to work. His mother washes. He didn't know what to do nor how to act. He kept his hands in his pockets most all the time. Aunt Lilly said it was shocking. But mother said, 'Never mind.' She said she was glad he had his pockets; for his hands were rough and not too clean, and she thought they mortified him. Father went and kissed her then. Don't tell this. I don't know what makes me run on and tell you all these things. I never spoke of them before. But I know father was a poor, young working man when he married mother."

The boy raised his hand, and the sparrow gave a twitter of delight and flew heavenward.

"Why," exclaimed Tommy in amazement, "you've cured him! He is all right. How did you do it? Do you feel sorry for the sparrows as well as Bob?"

"I pity every sparrow that is hurt," said the boy, "and isn't Bob of more consequence than a sparrow?"

"I wish," said Tommy, "I hadn't fought with Bob. It was most all my fault. I've a good mind to tell him so. I wish I was better acquainted with you. If I played with such a boy as you are, now, I'd be better I am certain. Suppose you come after school nights and play in our yard. Never mind your clothes. Can't you come?"

"Yes, I will come if you want me to," answered the boy, looking steadfastly at him a moment; "but now I must be about my father's business."

He stooped, lifted the bag of tools to his shoulders, and before Tommy could stay him had moved some steps away.

"Don't go yet, tell me some more about what you'd do," and Tommy turned to follow him.

But was it the boy? And was that a bag of tools on his back? It had grown strangely longer and heavier now, so that it dragged on the ground, and the face was the face of the Picture, and lo, it turned toward him, and the hand was raised in benediction and farewell, "I am with you always," and he was gone.

"Oh! come back, come back," sobbed Tommy, reaching out his arms and struggling to run after him.

"Poor boy," said his mother, wiping the blinding tears from his eyes, "your sleep didn't do you much good."

"I've not been asleep," said Tommy; "I've been talking with—with—Him," and he spoke low with a longing reverence and pointed to the Picture.

"It was a dream, my child."

"Mother, it was a vision. I saw Him, when He was a little boy in His own town, Nazareth. And, mother, I even told Him it wasn't much of a place to live in. He talked to me about Bob. He said you knew Him. I saw him cure a little bird. And oh, mother, He said He would be with me always. He is a little boy like me! I know what to do now. He showed me. I must find Bob; I must have him forgive me. I want to bring him home with me into my bed for to-night."

He stopped. "Mother," he said solemnly, "to-morrow is His birthday."

A NAZARETH CHRISTMAS

"Now, tell us, mother, again—as ever this night—the story of our brother's birth."

"Yes, dear mother, and not forgetting the star; for us no story is like this, not even the story of young King David, although in truth, that is a goodly tale."

"Then sit, children; lend me your aid with the gifts; and now, as dark comes on, while yet your father and brother are not returned from their work, I will repeat again the oft-told story. I see not how I can forget aught, for it seems ever before me.

"You must know it was between the wet time and the dry when your father and I went up to Judea to be enrolled. Bethlehem was our city. There were a great many journeying in our company to the House of Bread. I was not strong in those days; and so your father obtained an ass for me to ride, while he walked by my side. We traveled slowly, and the early night had already set in when we passed where Rachel rests, and reached the village. In front of the inn at which your father intended stopping, he left my side a moment, while he went to arrange for our stay; but he straightway returned, saying there was no room for us. So we were compelled to go farther; and it was late,—how late I know not,—before we found rest; for at every inn where your father knocked the answer was the same: 'No room!' 'No room!' Your father bore up bravely, though he had the harder part; while, in my childishness, I was fain to kneel in the chalk-dust of the road, and seek what rest I could. But he upheld me, until, at last, one inn-keeper, seeing what a child I was in truth took pity on me and said:

"I am able to do no more for you than for my poor cattle; but I can give you shelter with them in the cavern stable and a bed if only straw."

"And, children, I was very thankful for this. I had been told before that to me a Prince should be born; that, girl as I was, as mother, should clasp in

"

my arms a Savior-child. I believed the words of the angel,—for was I not of the house of David?—and ever treasured them in my heart. Now, how strange should it be that not in my peaceful Nazareth, not in this, our own home, but: there, and that weary night of all nights, beside me on the straw should be laid my infant son!

"I knew immediately what to call him, for, as I have often told you, the angel had named him 'Jesus.' 'Even so,' the angel had said; 'for he shall save his people from their sins.' I have wondered much what that means for your brother."

"Watch well your work, children! Burn not the cakes. Fold with care the mantles and the coats. This garment we will lay aside for patches. It repays not labor to put new to old; and, James, test well the skins before you fill them with the wine. We know not to whom your brother bears the gifts of his handiwork to-night, but he knows who needs them most, and naught must be lost or wasted.

"Where was I in the story, children?"

"The baby on the hay, sweet mother."

"Ah, yes, I mind me now. I took him in my arms. To me no child had ever looked the same. But now, a marvel! The rock stable, which before had seemed dark indeed, lighted only by our dim lamps, suddenly shone full of light. I raised my eyes, and there, before and above me, seemingly through a rent in the roof, I beheld a most large and luminous star. Verily, I had not seen the opening in the roof when I had lain me down, but now I could do naught else but look from my baby's face beside me, along the floods of light to the star before.

"And now, without, rose a cry: 'We are come to behold the King. We are guided.' And, entering the stable, clad in their coats of sheepskin, with their slings and crooks yet in their hands, came shepherds, I cannot now recall the number."

"I had wrapped my babe in his clothes, and had lain him in his manger. And now it was so that as soon as their eyes fell upon his face, they sank to their knees and worshiped him."

"'Heard you not,' spake a white-bearded shepherd to me; 'heard you not, young Mother Mary, the angels' song?'"

"'Meseems I have long heard it, and can hear naught else, good father,' I answered."

"To us it came,' he said, 'in the first watch of this night, and with it music not of earth.'"

"Afterward came the learned ones from the Eastern countries,—I know not now the land.

The gifts they brought him made all the place seem like a king's palace; and with all their gifts they gave him worship also."

"And I lay watching it all. And it shall be always so, I thought."

"But these, though wise men, were not of our race, and could not follow the guiding star with our faith.

Wherefore, so much stir had they made throughout the kingdom, inquiring publicly concerning this, your brother, that, through the jealousy of Herod, great was the trouble and misery that fell upon the innocent after their going."

"But hearken, children; I hear even now your father and your brother coming from their work. Place quickly the gifts within the basket."

It is a gentle figure that bends among mother and children, and a tender voice that questions:

"Shall I bear forth the gifts?"

"They are ready now, my son. Even this moment thy brother James placed the last within the basket, but canst thou not partake of the evening meal before thou goest with them? Thou art but a lad, to go forth alone after a day of toil."

"Nay, but I must be about the Master's work; and, look, the stars are rising. I should tarry not, for they who toil long rest early."

"For whom is thy service to-night, my son? Last birth-night it was to the sorrowing; before that to the blind, and even yet to the deaf and the lame. And whither tend thy footsteps now?"

"To the tempted ones, mother."

"And thou shalt stay their feet, dear boy, for rememberest not the Immanuels of last year? How the sorrowful found strange, staying joy in their hearts?

How the blind said, as thou named their gifts, and placed them in their hands, that it seemed they could straightway behold them?

How even the dumb gave forth pleasant sounds like music from their helpless tongues? and how even the lame well-nigh leaped from their lameness, for the light of thy young face?

But when thou comest to thy crown and throne thou needest not got forth alone upon thy birth-night, but send out thy gifts with love and plenty."

"I know not, my mother."

"But all will be thine? What said the angel: 'The Lord God shall give unto him the throne of his father David; and of his kingdom there shall be no end!' It may be soon, we know not, for lo! King David was but a boy, and at his daily toil, when he was called to reign over the house of Jacob. Forget not, thou art born the King."

"Oh, gladden not thy heart, loved mother, with this joy. I seek not to behold the future, but I see not in this world my kingdom, for the rose blossoms I pluck from out the hedge-rows fall; and it is their thorn branch that ever within my hands twines into a crown."